P9-BZQ-257

THE TEACHER WHO
Forgot Too Much

by
Steve Brezenoff

★

illustrated by
C.B. Canga

STONE ARCH BOOKS
www.stonearchbooks.com

Field Trip Mysteries are published by Stone Arch Books,
A Capstone Imprint
151 Good Counsel Drive, P.O. Box 669
Mankato, Minnesota 56002
www.capstonepub.com

Copyright © 2010 by Stone Arch Books

Library of Congress Cataloging-in-Publication Data
Brezenoff, Steven.
   The teacher who forgot too much / by Steve Brezenoff ;
illustrated by C.B. Canga.
        p. cm. — (Field trip mysteries)
   ISBN 978-1-4342-1609-0
   [1. School field trips—Fiction. 2. Mystery and detective
stories.] I. Canga, C. B., ill. II. Title.
   PZ7.B7576Te 2010
   [Fic]—dc22
        2009002573

Printed in the United States of America in Stevens Point, Wisconsin.
072013   007593R

PRINTED IN
THE U.S.A.

Creative Director:
          Heather Kindseth
Graphic Designer:
          Carla Zetina-Yglesias

Summary:
Catalina "Cat" Duran and her class are
off to the recycling center for what seems
like the worst field trip ever. But when
they arrive, they find out that the recycling
plant has been sabotaged! Only Cat and
her friends can save the day (and help save
the Earth, too)!

Dear pa

The si

We v
We'
fro

D

★ TABLE OF CONTENTS ★

Catalina Duran

A.K.A: Cat

D.O.B: February 15th

POSITION: 6th Grade

INTERESTS:

Animals, being "green", field trips

KNOWN ASSOCIATES:

Archer, Samantha; Garrison, Edward; and Shoo, James. *Are these students spending too much time together?*

NOTES:

Catalina is well liked by most of her teachers and fellow students. *Sounds like a troublemaker.*

CHAPTER
ONE

My name is
Catalina Duran,
but everyone calls me
Cat –
like the cute and fuzzy animal.
Not that I'm fuzzy.

Anyway, my best friends and I have been through some crazy days. The weird thing is what happens on field trip days. Whenever we go on a field trip, it seems like something's always getting stolen or being wrecked or going missing.

For some reason, my friends and I have a knack for solving these crimes!

Who are my friends? Well, I have three best friends. Samantha Archer, who we all call Sam. James Shoo, who we all call Gum. And Edward Garrison, who we all call Egg. What can I say? We like nicknames.

The day I'm here to tell you about started out as a totally normal Tuesday morning. I was sitting on the school's front steps with Gum.

"Is it Friday yet?" Gum asked.

I laughed and said, "It's only Tuesday, Gum. Not even close to Friday."

Gum and I are usually the first of the bunch to get to school. We both live close to school, so we walk. It only takes me about five minutes, and Gum's walk isn't much longer.

Just then, Sam and Egg's bus pulled up. The brakes made a very loud squeak. Gum and I both covered our ears.

Sam and Egg were the very last ones off the bus. They always sit together all the way in the back.

"Good morning, you two," Egg said. He pulled his camera to his eye and snapped a quick shot of me and Gum. Egg takes his camera everywhere he goes.

"Good morning," I replied.

Egg glanced at his watch. "Let's get to class," he said. "I don't want Mr. Neff to leave without us!"

"Leave without us?" I asked. "What are you talking about?"

"He really might!" Sam said. "Mr. Neff is so absentminded, he probably would forget us here."

James laughed. "Yeah," he said. "Remember that time he showed up in a suit, but forgot to put a shirt on?"

I giggled. "He looked pretty funny with that jacket and tie on," I added.

A few minutes later, we were walking to Mr. Neff's science class. We have science with Mr. Neff every Tuesday morning.

Other mornings, we have different classes, like art or music or gym. The rest of the time we're in our regular class with Mr. Spade, our sixth-grade teacher.

Mr. Spade was leading us through the halls to Mr. Neff's science room. You could smell Mr. Neff's science room from miles away. It stinks like chemicals! I don't mind the smell though. I like science class. And I really like Mr. Neff.

Mr. Neff loves animals as much as I do, I think. Plus, he's always teaching us new ways to be green and to help the environment. He's even on some special city committee to make sure our town recycles and stays green.

One day he told us that he had helped the committee win a big lawsuit against the town landfill.

They had made it illegal for anything that could be recycled to go to the landfill. That meant our town had to recycle a lot of stuff instead of just throwing it away. I thought that was pretty cool.

"So," I said to Sam as we walked, "what was Egg talking about before? About Mr. Neff leaving without us?"

"Don't you remember, Cat?" Sam replied. "Field trip today!"

I thought for a moment. "Oh that's right!" I said. "The city recycling plant. I can't believe I forgot!"

Sam nodded. "Yup," she said. "I figured you'd be so excited."

"I am!" I replied. I really was. I don't know how I forgot. But this field trip to the recycling plant was a big deal for me.

Mr. Neff taught us a lot about recycling. He said that the world would be a better place if we didn't have to recycle — if we all stopped using stuff made out of plastic, and only used things that were biodegradable.

But until then, he said, recycling was a great thing to do.

Like I said, I love animals. And anything that helps animals — which includes recycling — I also love.

So I was very excited when Sam reminded me about the trip.

"Do you think they'll show us how the plastic is recycled and used to make carpets?" I asked. "Oh, I hope so!"

The others shrugged.

"Maybe we'll see aluminum cans being melted into fresh aluminum," I added. "Aluminum is very easy to recycle. That would be amazing!"

My friends just looked at me. For some reason, they just didn't seem as excited as I was.

"Well, I don't care what you guys say," I finally said. "This is an awesome field trip!"

But I had no idea how exciting that field trip would actually be.

THE LONG ROAD

"Okay, everyone," Mr. Neff said as the bus bounced along. "Let's do attendance so we know we're not missing anyone."

"Attendance now?" Gum whispered to me. The four of us were sitting in the two back seats. I was sitting in one seat with Gum, and Sam and Egg were across the aisle.

"What's the problem?" I asked.

"Isn't it too late if we did forget someone?" Gum said.

I laughed. "Yep," I said. "Plus, Mr. Neff can never remember our names anyway!"

Mr. Neff glanced around the bus. "I'll start in the back," he said, glancing at me and my friends.

Now, to be fair, we all love Mr. Neff. He's very nice and very funny. He is also the only teacher who uses our nicknames instead of our real names. That's pretty cool. The problem is, he can never remember what our nicknames are!

"Okay, Kit?" he said. He was looking right at me.

No one replied.

"Um," Mr. Neff tried again, still looking at me. "Dog?"

I slowly raised my hand. "You mean Cat, Mr. Neff?" I asked.

Mr. Neff looked confused, but then he smiled. "That's right, Cat," he said.

"Here," I replied with a smile.

It went on like that for the rest of the ride. He called Gum "Candy," and Egg "Cheese," then "Milk." He did manage to get Sam's name right on the first try, though.

For the millionth time, Mr. Neff said,

"Sorry about that, everyone. I'm great with faces, just awful with names!"

Just as the bus was pulling up to the recycling plant, a baseball hit the floor of the bus and bounced up to the front. It hit Mr. Neff right in the foot. Egg snapped a quick picture.

"Huh?" Mr. Neff said, bending over to get it. "What's this?"

"It's mine, Mr. Neff," Anton Gutman replied. He's the class meanie. He makes fun of everyone all the time. He's always causing trouble for the teachers.

"Why do you have a baseball with you, Andrew?" Mr. Neff asked, walking down the bus aisle to Anton's seat.

"Anton," Anton said, correcting him.

"Right," Mr. Neff said impatiently. "Why do you have a baseball?"

"Actually," Anton said, smiling, "I have three baseballs." He reached out and took the ball back from Mr. Neff.

"Why?" Mr. Neff asked. I could tell that he was getting annoyed.

"They're for our baseball game after school," Anton told him. "That one just fell out of my bag. It was an accident."

"Don't let it happen again," Mr. Neff said. Then the bus stopped. Everyone quickly stood up.

"Okay, everyone off," Mr. Neff announced.

We all piled onto the sidewalk in front of the plant. Just then, a man came running out of the plant.

"The field trip is off!" the man yelled.

"What?" Mr. Neff asked. All of us students stood there, shocked.

"Sorry, everyone," the man replied. "No field trip! The city recycling plant is closed — maybe for good!"

THE TRIP IS OFF!

"We planned this field trip months ago," Mr. Neff said. "You can't cancel it now that we're here."

The man patted his sweaty forehead with a hanky. "Are you Mr. Neff, the science teacher?" he asked.

"That's right," Mr. Neff replied. "What is the problem exactly?" Mr. Neff peeked around the tall man to try to look inside the plant.

"Mr. Neff, I'm Joe Astor," the man said. He stuck out his hand and Mr. Neff shook it. "I'm the shift supervisor."

"It's nice to meet you, Mr. Astor," Mr. Neff replied. "I wish you'd tell me the problem."

"Well," Mr. Astor said, "several machines in the plant suddenly broke down this morning."

"Broke down?" Gum asked. "How?"

Mr. Astor glanced at Gum and shrugged. "We don't know," the supervisor said. "But our new manager is very angry. It's his first day working at the recycling plant, and everything is going wrong! I can't bring a class of sixth graders through right now."

Mr. Neff leaned forward and spoke more quietly. "Listen," he said. "Suppose we just take them through very quickly. They can see the machines, even if nothing is working."

Mr. Astor frowned. "I don't know," he said slowly.

"The new manager won't even know we're here," Mr. Neff said. He smiled slyly.

Mr. Astor thought a moment. "Okay," he said in a whisper. "I'll walk you through, but we have to be quick!"

The whole class cheered. Mr. Astor jumped about ten feet.

"And quiet!" he shouted. "Tell your students to be quiet!"

THE PLANT MANAGER

The class followed Mr. Neff and Mr. Astor as quietly as we could into the recycling plant. We walked into a big room. It had a couple of nice couches, and thick green carpeting. There were several closed doors. There were three desks in the room, too. Each one had a small computer on it. Each desk also had a person's name on it. One of them belonged to Mr. Astor.

The last student into the plant's lobby closed the front door very quietly.

"Thank you for letting us in, Mr. Astor,"
I whispered. I was right up in front.

The sweaty supervisor glanced at me
and smiled. His face was bright red. I could
see he was having a very bad day.

"You're welcome, young lady," he replied
in a whisper.

Mr. Astor looked up at the rest of the
class. "This is the front office lobby area,"
he said in a slightly louder whisper. "We
have to be very, very quiet in here," he
added.

"How come?" Egg whispered, standing
next to me. I'm sure no one else in the class
heard him ask.

"The plant manager's office is right
through that door," Mr. Astor replied in his
quietest voice yet.

Mr. Astor pointed at a very fancy-looking wooden door across the room. It had golden trim and an engraved nameplate. The nameplate said "Mr. Greenstreet."

Suddenly I heard someone giggling behind me. I glanced over my shoulder.

Anton Gutman and two of his weaselly friends were standing together in the back of the group. They were laughing.

Sam leaned over to me, eyeing the group of troublemakers. "Thick as thieves, those three," she said.

Sam's always saying weird things like that. She hears them in the old movies she watches with her grandparents. She lives with her grandma and grandpa. But before I could even ask what she meant, I heard a loud thud.

Behind us, Anton and his friends nearly fell over laughing. I looked around and spotted a baseball bouncing away from the manager's fancy office door. I guess that's what had made the loud noise.

The ball bounced right under Mr. Astor's desk. I doubt anyone but me and Sam even noticed it happen.

But everyone had heard the loud thud — including the plant manager.

Suddenly the fancy door flew open. A man came storming out. He was wearing a big hat and had a very funny mustache.

"What in the world was that?" he shouted angrily.

Then he stopped in his tracks. He had noticed the big group of sixth graders.

Mr. Astor tried to smile. I heard him swallow nervously.

The manager stood over us and looked at each of us, one by one. Quietly, Egg snapped a quick photo.

"Sir," Mr. Astor said. "This is Mr. Neff's sixth-grade class."

The manager stared at Mr. Astor. Mr. Astor turned bright red.

"Their field trip is today," Mr. Astor added.

"That's right," Mr. Neff said. "We've been looking forward to it.

"Field trip," the manager muttered. "I see."

Then he glared at Mr. Neff. For a moment, I thought the manager would start shouting again. But instead, he suddenly smiled and quickly walked over to Mr. Neff.

"Mr. Neff!" the manager said very pleasantly. "Why, it's a pleasure to meet you!"

Mr. Neff smiled in return and shook the manager's hand. "The pleasure is mine," Mr. Neff said. "But for some reason, I think we've met before. I just can't remember where."

The manager thought for a moment. "Really?" he asked.

Mr. Neff nodded. "I'm certain," he said. "I never forget a face! Ask my class."

We all nodded to support our teacher. He was bad at names, but we all knew he was great at remembering faces.

"Mr. Dallas, isn't it?" Mr. Neff said.

The manager shook his head.

"Hmm, Mr. Austin, perhaps?" Mr. Neff tried again.

"Nope. My name is Mr. Greenstreet, and I don't think we've met before," the manager said.

Mr. Neff seemed confused. "I was sure it was Dallas or Austin," he muttered to himself. "Or maybe Arlington . . . ?"

"Well, enjoy your visit with us, class," Mr. Greenstreet said. "I need to get back to work. Oh, and did Mr. Astor tell you that most of the machines are broken? The plant isn't running today."

"Yes," Mr. Neff replied. "I'm sorry the kids won't see the plant in action."

Mr. Greenstreet shrugged. "Can't be helped," he said. With that, he walked back into his office. Then he slammed the door behind him.

TURNED AWAY

I have to say, the tour of the plant wasn't all that interesting. I mean, it was cool to see the piles of plastic here, and metal there, and paper over there. But with no machines whirring or materials being processed, there wasn't much to see.

Even the plant workers were mainly standing around. Egg took some photos of the stopped machines and the workers standing near them, but even Egg was bored. And he's hardly ever bored when he has his camera.

By the time lunch came along, we were all glad to go out to the picnic area and get some air. Mr. Neff stayed inside to talk to Mr. Astor.

"This is the worst field trip ever," Gum said as he unpacked his lunch. "What a waste of a day!"

Sam shrugged. "It's better than sitting in a hot classroom," she said.

"I guess," Gum agreed.

While we were eating our sandwiches, a loud truck pulled up at the loading bay nearby. Its engine chugged and sputtered to a stop. Then the driver hopped out.

Just then, Mr. Astor came jogging out of the loading bay door. "Hold it!" he cried. "Just a moment, please!"

"What's the problem, Joe?" the driver asked. He was ready to dump a big load of recyclables into the loading area. Then the bottles and cans and whatever else was in the truck would be sorted and brought inside the plant.

"We're too backed up in there," Mr. Astor said. "All of the machines have stopped working. We can't take any more recyclables today."

The driver scratched his head. "What am I supposed to do with this load?" he asked, pointing at his truck.

Mr. Astor took a deep breath and wiped the sweat from his brow. "I'm afraid you'll just have to take it all over to Houston's," he said.

The driver frowned. "Houston's Landfill? They don't take recyclables over there."

"Well, they do today," Mr. Astor said. He quickly fanned his face with his hand. "Mr. Greenstreet arranged it."

"If you say so," the driver said. He got back into his truck and started it up. "I'll see you soon, Joe."

Mr. Astor waved. Then the big truck drove off.

SABOTAGE!

By the time the noise of the loud truck driving away faded, lunch was over.

"Okay, class," Mr. Neff said, coming outside. "We're going to head back to school now."

"All good things must come to an end, I guess," Sam said.

The four of us got up from our table and tossed our empty wrappers into a nearby trashcan.

Then, as we went back into the plant to leave through the front door, Mr. Astor came running toward us. He was holding something in his hand.

"Stop!" he shouted at us. "Don't you kids leave yet!"

Mr. Neff turned. "What is it, Mr. Astor?" he asked.

Mr. Astor ran up to us and caught his breath. "Look what the maintenance crew just found in one of our broken machines!" he yelled.

He held up a baseball. It was badly scarred and torn up, but it was definitely a baseball.

Egg quickly snapped a photo of the torn-up ball.

Mr. Neff frowned at Mr. Astor. "I hope you're not suggesting one of my students had something to do with the broken machines!" Mr. Neff said.

Mr. Astor gasped. "I certainly am," he said. "The machine in question was one of the few that was actually working fine before your students got here."

Mr. Neff turned and faced Anton. "Andrew," Mr. Neff said, "Did you throw a baseball into a machine?"

"My name is Anton!" the troublemaker replied. "And no, I didn't."

Gum stepped up to Anton. "We all saw your baseball on the bus, Anton," Gum said. "It had to be you!"

"Let me see your bag," Mr. Neff said to Anton. He grabbed Anton's bag.

Anton looked around. "Okay," he said. He handed Mr. Neff his backpack.

Mr. Neff reached in and soon pulled out two baseballs. "Where's the third one?" he asked.

Anton smiled. "What third one?" he said smugly.

"On the bus you told me you had three baseballs for your game after school," Mr. Neff replied. "So where's the third?"

Anton shrugged. "I must have been wrong," he said. "I guess I only had two."

"He's lying!" Mr. Astor said. He held up the torn-up baseball. Then he said, "This is the third one! That boy sabotaged our machine."

"You're going to be in big trouble when we get back to school, young man," Mr. Neff told Anton. "Unless you can show me where that third baseball is, I'm afraid I can't think of any other explanation!"

CHAPTER SEVEN

UNSOLVED?

Sam and I glanced at each other.

"I can't believe we're about to do this," I said.

"I know," Sam agreed. "We're going to clear Anton Gutman's name."

We both shook our heads, but we had to be honest.

"Mr. Neff," I said. "Anton did have three baseballs."

"But the one Mr. Astor has isn't one of them," Sam added.

"What? What are you girls talking about?" Mr. Neff asked.

Egg and Gum glanced at us. "Yeah," Gum said, "what are you two talking about?"

"We'll show you," I replied. I took Sam by the arm. Together, we walked into the lobby. Mr. Neff and Mr. Astor followed us, and the rest of the class followed them.

"It went under there," Sam said. She pointed to Mr. Astor's desk.

I got down on all fours near the desk. I reached around under the desk, but I couldn't find anything. I scooched down as far as I could and reached as far back under the desk as I could. Nothing.

"I don't get it," I said, jumping to my feet. "That's where the ball went."

Anton walked up. "Um, didn't you find it?" he asked, looking at me.

I shrugged and shook my head.

Sam got down on her knees and looked under the desk. "I'm sure that's where it went," she said. "I saw it roll under there!"

"It did!" Anton said. He looked worried. "I saw it too!"

"Weird," Sam said. I nodded. How could a baseball just disappear?

Anton spun to face Mr. Neff. "I swear, Mr. Neff," he said. "That's the last time I saw the third baseball."

"What is this all about?" Mr. Neff asked. "What are we looking for?" He looked at me and Sam.

I glanced at Sam. We might not like Anton Gutman, but we're not tattlers. I didn't want to tell Mr. Neff what Anton had done with the ball before it rolled under there.

I looked at Anton. He swallowed. I waited.

"Mr. Neff," Anton finally said, "I did have another baseball. When we first got here, I threw it at the manager's office door. Then it rolled under that desk, like Cat and Sam said."

Mr. Neff frowned. "Why did you do that?" he asked Anton.

Anton shrugged and looked at his feet. Usually, his pranks never got found out. He always got away with everything. Now, he looked pretty upset. "It was just a joke," he replied. "I thought it would be funny."

"Well, it wasn't funny," Mr. Neff said. He turned to Mr. Astor. "I'll deal with my students, Mr. Astor," Mr. Neff told him. "But unfortunately, anyone could have picked up that baseball after Andrew lost it."

"My name is Anton," Anton said, correcting Mr. Neff.

"Right," Mr. Neff said. "I'm sorry Anton brought that baseball into your plant, Mr. Astor, but it seems he knows nothing about the sabotage."

Mr. Astor huffed and puffed. His face turned redder and redder. "Well, someone has broken our machines!" he said angrily, shaking his fist at us. "And I am going to find out who it was!"

With that, the supervisor stormed back into the main part of the plant.

Mr. Neff turned and looked at us. I could tell he was very disappointed.

"Do you think we should get back on the bus, Mr. Neff?" Egg asked.

Mr. Neff glanced at his watch. "It's earlier than we were supposed to leave," he said. "I better call the bus driver to let him know we're ready to head back. You kids stay here in the lobby."

He walked off to find a phone.

"So who do you guys think sabotaged the machines?" Sam asked.

Gum stroked his chin. "I'll solve this mystery," he said. "Just give me a minute."

Egg looked around carefully to make sure no one was listening. Then he whispered, "I think it was Mr. Neff."

"Mr. Neff?"

I said, practically shouting.

"Are you crazy?"

Egg shook his head. "No, I'm not crazy. Don't you remember what he said in class?" he asked.

"You mean that he hates plastics?" Sam asked.

Egg nodded. "Right," he said. "If the recycling plant stops working, people might stop using plastic. Since Mr. Neff said it's illegal for the landfill to take recyclable stuff, then people would have to use things that could go to the landfill."

"Things that are biodegradable, you mean," I said.

"Right," said Egg.

"I don't know," Gum said. "I mean, today Houston's Landfill is taking recyclables."

"That's true," I said.

"Maybe they're just storing them and they'll bring them back when the recycling plant opens again, but I doubt it," Gum went on. "And I bet if the recycling plant was closed for good, it wouldn't be illegal to bring plastic to the landfill."

I added, "Mr. Neff seems to be glad we can recycle the plastic things, even if he doesn't much like them to begin with."

Egg put up his hands. "I still think it's Mr. Neff," he said. "He seems so distracted, and he has the motive. Stop the recycling plant so people can't use plastic."

"Mr. Neff always seems distracted," I said. "That's nothing new."

"I'm still not ruling out Anton," Gum said. "Just because he dropped the baseball doesn't mean he didn't go back later and pick it up."

"The baseball was under Mr. Astor's desk," I pointed out. "Maybe he found it."

Just then, Mr. Neff came back into the lobby. "Okay, class," he said. "The bus will be out front in a moment. Let's head out there and get in line, please."

"I guess we're not going to solve this mystery," I said sadly.

"But we have to solve it!" Gum said as we headed out the front door. "We always solve the mysteries!"

Sam sighed. "We don't even have one clue," she said. "How can we?"

That moment, another loud truck chugged up to the plant.

HOUSTON'S FORTUNE

Mr. Astor ran outside. "Stop!" he shouted at the driver. "Don't pull that truck in. The plant is not accepting any materials today. The machinery has been sabotaged."

"The plant's been sabotaged?" the driver asked, shocked.

Mr. Astor nodded. "That's right," he said. "So until we find out who broke the machines, everything has to go to Houston's Landfill instead."

"Houston's Landfill," I said quietly. "I wonder . . ."

"Wonder what, Cat?" Sam asked.

"Mr. Astor!" I said, jogging over to him. "Can I ask you a question?"

The driver of the recycling truck went back to his truck. Mr. Astor turned to me and wiped his brow.

"What is it, young lady?" Mr. Astor said. "I'm very busy."

"Well," I said quickly, "how come Houston's Landfill is taking all the recycling?"

"Where else would it go?" he replied. "It can't fit in the plant with the machines broken. And the drivers can't keep it on the trucks."

Egg stepped up beside me. "But Mr. Neff told us that landfills are not allowed to accept recyclables," he added.

"Right," I said. "It would be like putting a tin can in your compost pile!"

Mr. Astor looked at his watch. Then he glanced over at a nearby window. We saw Mr. Greenstreet, the plant manager, watching us.

"I don't have time to stand here and chat about it. Since the recycling plant is closed, the city made a deal with the landfill," Mr. Astor said.

"What kind of deal?" I asked.

"Houston's Landfill will take the recyclables until the recycling plant is up and running again," Mr. Astor said. "The city agreed to make it legal again and to pay double their normal fee. Mr. Houston must be making a fortune today!" He shook his head and walked off.

"Double their fee?" Egg said, shocked.

"And it's not illegal for them to take recyclables anymore," I said. "I think we found our motive."

Sam and Gum walked up to us.

"We have to get on the bus," Sam said.

"Tell Mr. Neff to wait," I said. "I think we just solved this mystery."

THANK YOU AND GOODBYE

"Kit!" Mr. Neff said. "Cheese! The bus needs to leave now. We're waiting for you."

I laughed. "It's Cat and Egg!" I said. "Not Kit and Cheese!"

"I can't keep track of these crazy names," Mr. Neff said. "But we have to get on the bus now."

"Just one minute, Mr. Neff," I said. "I want to say thank you and goodbye to the plant manager."

I rushed back into the lobby and knocked on Mr. Greenstreet's door.

"We don't have time for this, Kitty!" Mr. Neff said as he ran after me. "Leave Mr. Arlington alone!"

Egg jogged up next to me. "What are you up to, Cat?" he asked. "I don't think Mr. Greenstreet wants to be bugged right now. He seemed so angry before."

"I think Mr. Neff was closer when he said Arlington," I replied. "Or Dallas or Austin."

"Huh?" Mr. Neff said. "What's she talking about, Biscuit?" he asked Egg.

I banged on the office door again. Finally, it swung open.

"What is it?" the manager shouted. His mustache looked crooked.

"Sorry to bother you,
Mr. Houston,"
I said, smiling.
"I wanted to thank you
for letting us visit your plant."

"Yes, yes," the manager replied. His belly shook. "Don't mention it. Goodbye."

"Mr. Houston!" Mr. Neff suddenly shouted. "That's it! I knew we'd met before."

"What?" the manager said in a huff. "No, no. My name is Greensleeves. I mean, Greenstreet."

"Aha!" Egg said. "You're Mr. Houston, the owner of Houston's Landfill."

Mr. Neff frowned. "That's right," our teacher said. "I met you at the community board meeting. That's when we made it illegal for your landfill to accept any recyclables!"

He looked hard at the man and added angrily, "And your mustache is fake!"

The manager grumbled and started to say something, but instead he just stepped back into his office and closed the door. I heard the latch drop as he locked it from the inside.

Mr. Neff put a hand on my shoulder. "You sure cracked that case, Rabbit," he said.

Egg, or should I say "Cheese," and I laughed.

CASE CLOSED

Detective Jones showed up pretty quickly after Mr. Astor called the police.

"You kids again!" the detective said when he saw me, Egg, Gum, and Sam. "I think I'll have to make you honorary detectives before long," he added. "Who solved this one?"

Egg pointed at me. "It was Cat, detective," he said.

The detective looked at me. "So how did you figure it out?" he asked. "How did you know Mr. Greenstreet, the new plant manager, was actually Mr. Houston, the owner of Houston's Landfill, in disguise?"

"Well," I replied, "Mr. Neff really deserves the credit."

"Me?" Mr. Neff said. "What did I do?"

"You never get a name right," I said, "but you're always close!"

"Really?" Mr. Neff said, blushing. "I didn't know I did that."

"Sure," Egg said. "You call me 'Cheese' instead of 'Egg.'"

"And me 'Candy' instead of 'Gum,'" Gum added.

Sam and I laughed. "So," I went on, "when you called Mr. Greenstreet 'Dallas,' 'Austin,' and 'Arlington' . . ."

"All cities in Texas!" Sam pointed out.

I nodded. "Just like Houston," I finished, "the name of the landfill that is making extra money today because of the broken equipment! That's how I figured out that Mr. Houston did it."

The detective nodded slowly. "Brilliant work," he said.

"You'll make a fine addition to the force one day."

With that, he led Mr. Houston out of the lobby and into a police car.

"Another mystery solved," Gum said, clapping his hands together.

"And more importantly," I said, picking up a plastic water bottle from the ground, "Mr. Houston won't be able to stop this city from recycling."

Mr. Neff patted me on the back. "Good going, Cat," he said. "Or is it Puppy?"

The four of us laughed as our teacher stepped onto the bus.

"Think he'll get our names right before we finish the school year?" Sam asked.

"Not a chance, Pam," I said. "Not a chance."

literary news

MYSTERIOUS WRITER REVEALED!

► SAINT PAUL, MN

Steve Brezenoff lives in St. Paul, Minnesota, with his wife, Beth, their son, Sam, and their small, smelly dog, Harry. Besides writing books, he enjoys playing video games, riding his bicycle, and helping middle-school students work on their writing skills. Steve's ideas almost always come to him in his dreams, so he does his best writing in his pajamas.

arts & entertainment

CALIFORNIA ARTIST IS KEY TO SOLVING MYSTERY – POLICE SAY

Early on, C. B. Canga's parents discovered that a piece of paper and some crayons worked wonders in taming the restless dragon. There was no turning back. In 2002 he received his BFA in Illustration from the Academy of Arts University in San Francisco. He works at the Academy of Arts as a drawing instructor. He lives in California with his wife, Robyn, and his three kids.

A Detective's Dictionary

force (FORSS)—short for police force, a group of police officers who work together

fortune (FOR-chuhn)—a lot of money or treasure

honorary (HON-or-air-ee)—given as an honor without the usual requirements or duties

knack (NAK)—a skill for something

motive (MOH-tiv)—a reason for doing something

prank (PRAYNK)—a trick

sabotage (SAB-uh-tahj)—secretly ruin

slyly (SLY-lee)—sneakily

thick as thieves (THIK AZ THEEVZ)—very close friends who have no secrets from each other

Catalina Duran

Mr. Neff's Science Class

September 16

(A)

Fake Names

The man we met on our field trip is not the first person to use a false name. People have been using false names throughout history. Some people use false names to hide their identity, like Mr. Houston did.

False names don't have to be used to cover up criminal behavior. They can be used for other reasons, too. Some people use false names because their real names sound funny. Finally, some people use false names to help their careers.

Some people use false names if they are important leaders. For example, Queen Vict... was the queen of England from 1837 to 190... Her name wasn't Victoria. It was Alexandr... Victoria of Kent.

Many writers have used false names. Mark Twain is one of the most famous fake names in American literature. His real name was Samuel Clemens. The writer Stephen King published some books using the name Richard Bachman.

Today, we know of many people who use false names. Some people choose new names that sound cooler or more interesting. Some choose names that are meaningful to them. Most people who choose new names do it because they want to change their names, not because they are trying to hide something, like Mr. Houston was.

Very interesting paper, Catalina! Good work.
—Mr. Neff (P.S. Did you know that nicknames are a kind of false name? That means you and your friends each use false names too.)

FURTHER INVESTIGATIONS

CASE #FTM02CD

1. In this book, Mr. Neff took our class on a field trip to the recycling plant. Where have you gone on a field trip? If you could go anywhere on a field trip, where would you choose to go?

2. Recycling is important to me for a lot of reasons. What do you think about recycling?

3. Gum, Egg, Sam, and I made a list of suspects to solve this mystery. Think of a mystery that needs to be solved at your school or home. Working as a group, make a list of suspects. Then solve the mystery!

1. Anton Gutman is always causing trouble. Write about a troublemaker you know. What does that person do to cause trouble?

2. In this book, Mr. Houston wore a disguise and gave himself a fake name. Draw a picture of yourself with a disguise. Then choose a fake name for yourself.

3. This book is a mystery story. Write your own mystery story!

THEY SOLVE CRIMES, CATCH CROOKS, CRACK CODES . . . AND RIDE THE BUS BACK TO SCHOOL AFTERWARD.

Meet Egg, Gum, Sam, and Cat.
Four sixth-grade detectives and best
friends. Wherever field trips take them,
mysteries aren't far behind . . .

FIELD TRIP 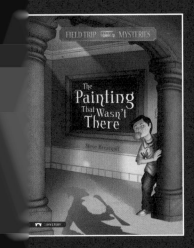 MYSTERIES

The Painting That Wasn't There

Steve Brezenoff

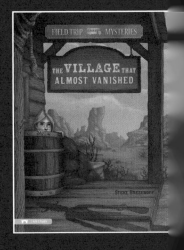

THE VILLAGE THAT ALMOST VANISHED

Steve Brezenoff

The TEACHER WHO Forgot Too Much

Steve Brezenoff

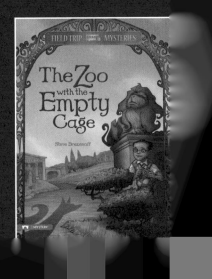

The Zoo with the Empty Cage

Steve Brezenoff

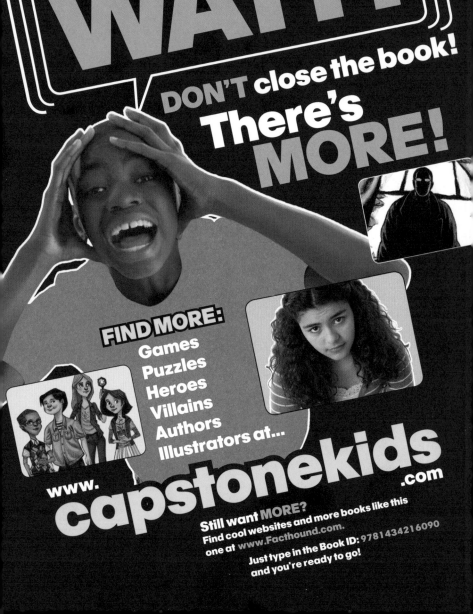